World's Worst Parrot

World's Worst Parrot

Alice Kuipers

orca currents

ORCA BOOK PUBLISHERS

Library and Archives Canada Cataloguing in Publication

Title: World's worst parrot / Alice Kuipers.
Names: Kuipers, Alice, 1979– author.
Series: Orca currents.
Description: Series statement: Orca currents

Identifiers: Canadiana (print) 20190169117 | Canadiana (ebook) 20190169125 |
ISBN 9781459823754 (softcover) | ISBN 9781459823761 (PDF) |
ISBN 9781459823778 (EPUB)

Classification: LCC PS8621.U38 W67 2020 | DDC jc813/.6—dc23

Library of Congress Control Number: 2019943972
Simultaneously published in Canada and the United States in 2020

Summary: In this high-interest novel for middle readers,
Ava's life suddenly becomes very complicated when
she inherits a troublesome African gray parrot.

*Orca Book Publishers is committed to reducing the consumption
of nonrenewable resources in the making of our books. We make
every effort to use materials that support a sustainable future.*

Orca Book Publishers gratefully acknowledges the support for its publishing
programs provided by the following agencies: the Government of Canada,
the Canada Council for the Arts and the Province of British Columbia
through the BC Arts Council and the Book Publishing Tax Credit.

Edited by Tanya Trafford
Design by Ella Collier
Cover artwork by gettyimages.ca/ekazansk
Author photo by Emma Love

ORCA BOOK PUBLISHERS
orcabook.com

Printed and bound in Canada.

23 22 21 20 • 4 3 2 1

To my son Theo

Chapter One

Ava sits on her white sheets. She leans over to fluff her blue pillows. She snaps a selfie. Then deletes it. *Yuck!* She pouts. Snap. Delete. Pout. Snap. *Perfect!* She draws squiggles and hearts around herself in the photo. She types some text on top:

Good morning! Beautiful day. Time for breakfast with the fam. Lucky me!

#homelife #perfect #Sundays

She posts it to her 542 followers. No! Now there are 543. Excellent! Her post isn't really true. There won't be any family breakfast today. There's never any time for that. Not since Dad left. This morning Mom is busy working in her home office. And Ava's stupid brother, Gregg, is still asleep.

Ava's phone flashes. She has two likes already. So what if her post isn't true? People *like* it. A couple more little hearts appear. Both of her BFFs post comments.

@journey314 You are soooo pretty Ava girl!!!

@purevision Breakfast with your hot brother. #swoon #luckyforsure #perfectfamily

Ava imagines herself as a famous online celebrity. She flies all over the world. She gets tons of free stuff. She goes to all the best parties and galas.

Ava is still daydreaming about her fantasy life when her mom comes into her room. She is wearing a gray suit, and her hair is freshly cut and colored. But her eyes are red. She has been crying.

"Honey, I have something to tell you," her mom says, not looking at Ava. She rearranges the one book that is out of place on Ava's white shelf.

"What's wrong?"

Ava's mom sighs. She pushes her hair back, and some of it sticks straight up. Ava notices that one of the buttons on her mom's suit is missing. Which is weird because even though she works at home, Ava's mom likes to look perfect. Right now she looks like a hot mess.

"This came in the mail on Friday. I didn't open it because I've been very busy." Her mom holds out an envelope with a handwritten address on it. "I actually thought it was a charity asking for money. I didn't think..."

3

She wipes her eyes. "Oh, just read it, would you?"

Ava takes the envelope and pulls out a letter. The paper is very thin. It has loopy handwriting on it. There are a few blotches.

Dear Ava,

I remember when you came to visit. You were seven. And so cute! You loved Mervin so much. It is my dying wish that you look after him well.

With all my love,
Great-Uncle Bertie

Her mom's phone buzzes. She checks it, sighs and glances at Ava. "I guess it's true. I just got a message from the lawyer. Great-Uncle Bertie is dead."

"Great-Uncle Bertie is dead?" Ava reads the words again. "Wait a minute. Who is Great-Uncle Bertie?"

"Nana's brother. You only met him once. He was very busy sailing all over the world. Huge traveler. No wife or kids. We met him in a hotel in London when we went to Europe. Remember, he had a room in that fancy hotel? That's where he lived when he wasn't at sea."

"I don't remember him at all."

"Well, he clearly remembers you!"

"What does he mean when he writes 'you loved Mervin so much'? *Who* is Mervin?"

"The lawyer says that Mervin is a parrot."

"A parrot?" Ava's face screws up. "Oh my god! I do remember. That old gray bird. Super grouchy, from what I remember. Surely that thing can't still be alive."

"Parrots live for years, Ava." Two tears fall down her mom's cheeks.

"I'm sorry, Mom. You must miss Uncle Bertie so much."

"No, that's not it. I hardly knew the old man. You don't understand. His parrot is coming to live with us. In *our* house."

"There's no way!"

"Listen, if you hadn't been so friendly with that bird, none of this would have happened. We can't have a parrot here."

She's totally right. A parrot would not look good on Ava's online profiles. She has a spotless, white room. The accent color is light blue. The feature image on the main wall is an anchor— Ava loves the sea. Well, she loves the *idea* of the sea. Living in a big city, she doesn't actually get to the ocean that much.

"We can say no, right?" Ava asks. "I don't know anything about parrots. I can't look after a parrot."

"I don't see how we can, honey." Her mom's eyes narrow. "It was Great-Uncle Bertie's dying wish." Her eyes become even more narrow, until they close. This is the face she pulls when she wants to shut out the world. She releases a slow breath. Ava knows she is counting to ten.

"I guess you're right, Mom."

"Great-Uncle Bertie is probably laughing in his grave."

Ava frowns. "Why?"

"He always said I was too obsessed with being neat and tidy. Too obsessed with image. Now he's putting a filthy bird in my house." She opens her eyes.

"There's nothing wrong with wanting a clean house. Or a good image."

Ava's mom smiles. "You are a girl after my own heart. We'll figure out how to stop that parrot from coming here. Dying wish or not. I'll message the lawyer." She taps on her phone.

Her phone buzzes in reply. She reads the screen, then holds it up for Ava to see.

Mervin already on his way. Express Post. Should arrive this afternoon. He's an African gray parrot. With a nasty bite!

"I'm *not* looking after a parrot, Mom!" Ava yells. "You have to stop this!"

There's a thud in the next room. It's Ava's big brother jumping out of bed. He appears at her doorway, scratching his chest. He's tall, with dark hair and eyes. Her BFFs think he's hot. Over the last year he has gone from being a skinny, annoying boy into the guy they all want to get to know. Ava can't understand what they see in him. Right now he's in worn-out sweats that are stained with coffee. He farts.

"Get out!" Ava yells.

"Not until I find out what's going on in here," Gregg says. He always has such a loud voice.

"Quality family time," says Ava sarcastically.

Their mom closes her eyes and breathes out.

"Seriously, what's all the yelling about?" Gregg asks. Even more loudly.

Ava holds out the letter. Gregg snatches it. He reads it and then collapses into laughter. "You're getting a parrot, Ava? Miss Prissy Pants?"

"What? Are you five years old? Don't call me that."

"We should put it right here. On your empty desk that looks so perfect because you never use it!" He falls onto Ava's bed, laughing harder.

Their mom squeezes her eyes more tightly shut.

"See?" Ava says to no one. "A perfect family Sunday."

Chapter Two

Ava hears the doorbell but doesn't move. She is never going to move again. She knows some people love animals. They are all about cute, fluffy pets. Their online feeds are full of adorable pet pictures. Ava scrolls through her phone. Maybe she could do adorable pet pictures. Maybe she could make Mervin the parrot into an internet superstar. Cute and adorable. Ava and Mervin.

Ava hears a loud squawk. Her mom yells, "Ava, come here!"

Gregg bursts into laughter. Again. He is such a jerk.

Ava gets off her bed. Opening her bedroom door, she sees a huge, fancy cage in the hall. It comes up to her chest, and it looks like it's made of gold. Inside, a scruffy parrot with beady eyes blinks at Ava.

"Wow. That cage is stunning. It's going to look amazing in my room!" Ava says.

"In your room, Monkey Face?" Gregg says. "I thought you said you were going to die if you had to be anywhere near the parrot."

"Well, I'm making the most of a bad situation." Ava sticks her tongue out at him. "And don't call me Monkey Face!"

The parrot lets out another really loud squawk. And Ava thought *Gregg* was loud. This bird just might burst her eardrums.

"Mervin! Hello!" Ava steps closer to the cage. The parrot cocks its head.

"MONKEY FACE!" it screeches.

Gregg explodes with laughter. "Monkey Face! That's right. That's her name!" He points at Ava and laughs again.

"Shut up, Gregg! You're such an idiot."

"IDIOT. MONKEY FACE!" says the bird. Then it squawks again.

"Stop it!" Ava cries.

Their mom, who was signing something for the delivery guy, comes over. She says, "He says we have to keep him for at least today. We can call the zoo tomorrow."

"The zoo!" says Gregg. "You can't send this bird to the zoo. You know it was Great-Uncle Bertie's dying wish that Ava care for this bird. She must look after it. She must love it!" He laughs again.

Ava thwacks him in the stomach.

"PRETTY," the bird says to their mom.

"Well, aren't you sweet?" she replies. "Maybe Gregg has a point. Perhaps we should at least try to honor Uncle Bertie's wish."

"I agree," Ava says. She is thinking about how nice the cage will look in her next online post. She imagines her followers falling in love with her adorable new pet.

"You *agree*?" Gregg asks.

"Absolutely. Can you pretty please help bring the cage into my bedroom?"

Gregg, who seems a bit stunned by Ava being so nice, picks up the cage.

"Actually, hang on, brother dear." Ava holds up her phone and frames a photo.

Mervin has one eye looking at the screen. Just behind her head. Ava purses her lips. The image of the two of them together makes for an interesting and beautiful photo. Perfect. She is about to snap the shot when Gregg stumbles.

"This thing is heavy!" he cries.

As the cage jolts, the latch on the cage door catches in Ava's hair. She screams in pain. The golden doorway yanks open as she drops her phone. There is a rustle of feathers. Then Mervin the parrot blasts out of the cage. He is so fast! And so big! He flies around the living room. "IDIOT MONKEY FACE, IDIOT MONKEY FACE!" Mervin yells.

Their mom screams. Gregg grabs Ava's phone. Ava is still trying to pull her hair free of the cage.

"Stop it, Gregg!"

He holds up her phone and takes a photo. He types on the screen.

"What are you doing?" Ava screams.

He reads out loud as he types, *"Welcoming our newest member of the fam! Hashtag Perfect Family Sunday.* That's your type of post, right, Ava?"

"Do *not* post that!" Ava detaches herself from the cage and runs toward him.

He holds the phone over his head. She jumps up. But Gregg is too tall now. Ava hits him. He laughs.

Mervin swoops. "MONKEY FACE! IDIOT!"

Their mom slides into an armchair. "Oh," she says. It sounds as if all the air has gone out of her.

Ava watches Mervin deposit bird poop directly on their mom's head.

"You are blowing up the internet, little sister!" Gregg yells. "It's already been liked thirty times! Yes! Now someone is sharing it!"

"What?"

Gregg is staring at Ava's phone, holding it above his head.

"What did you do?" Ava asks, panic in her eyes.

"Posted for you. I know you've always dreamed of being an internet superstar. Well, now you are!"

Gregg angles the phone so Ava can see. She still can't reach it from his outstretched hand.

But now she can see what everyone is seeing. The image is of Ava, mouth open, hair tangled in the cage door. Her eyes are as wide as her mouth. She looks *crazy*. And even more crazy-looking is the bird in the background. It is in midflight, beak pointed toward Ava, one eye perfectly in focus.

"Now that is a good photo, Monkey Face," Gregg says. "I don't know how I got that eyeball in focus like that. I mean, I must be a genius."

"You're a nightmare!" Ava shrieks.

"Gregg, give your sister her phone back," their mom says. She gets up from the armchair. "It is a good photo though. You're right. Perfect focus."

"What have you done?" Ava screams.

"A hundred likes, little sister! In, like, three minutes! And you have, wow, 665 followers now! I'm going to be your social media manager!"

"Gregg, stop!" Ava screams. Again. She keeps screaming, but her new reality isn't changing.

Mervin lands on Ava's head. She puts up both of her hands and staggers backward. "Mervin, off!"

Gregg brings the phone down and snaps another shot. "Got you! This is awesome!"

"What are you doing! No, Gregg, don't post anything else. Please!" Ava begs.

"Gregg, enough." Their mom puts her hands on her hips. She doesn't seem to have noticed the poop in her hair.

"This is for *you*, Ava! You're internet-famous. Like you always wanted. How's this? *My buddy birdy and me enjoying life. Hashtag avaandmervin.*"

Ava and Mervin. Hmm. Ava *had* been thinking of hashtags before Mervin landed on her head. Now she has bird claws digging into her scalp. Her brother is destroying her life. And her mom still looks like she's about to faint.

"We have to get this bird out of here, Mom!" Ava yells.

"No need to shout, honey. First we have to get the bird out of your hair."

Suddenly Mervin lifts off from Ava's head. He swoops to the top of the curtain rail. Poops again. On the curtain. Then he says in a sad voice, "HOME."

Gregg snorts. "He's like a feathery E.T."

"What's an E.T.?" Ava asks.

"A character in a great movie. You've never seen it? It's about an alien who just wants to go home. Like your bird. Here, Mervin," Gregg calls. He holds out an arm. "Poor guy. Come to Gregg."

The bird soars over. He lands on Gregg's arm.

While Gregg is distracted by the stupid bird, Ava grabs her phone.

How is it possible that she now has 801 followers? This is what she's always wanted. But right now she would rather die. She deletes both posts. But even as she does, someone shares screenshots of them, tagging her. These pictures are never going away.

Her life is over.

Chapter Three

Walking to school, Ava stays as far behind Gregg as possible. She hates him. She hates the parrot more. Gregg and their mom made her keep the horrible animal in her room last night. Their mom said they couldn't get rid of him because it was Sunday. There was nowhere to call—even the delivery people didn't answer their phone.

And after their mom discovered the poop in her hair and on the curtain, Mervin was banned from the living room.

Mervin squawked and called Ava "Monkey Face" all night long. She hardly slept, the bird was so noisy.

It is a cold gray day. As cold and gray as Ava feels inside.

There was another reason she was awake all night. Ava kept checking her phone.

She checks it again now. Almost *1,000* followers! And loads of messages asking for more #mervinandava pictures.

How can Ava even go to school? Her reputation is ruined.

As Gregg gets to the school doors, he turns and waves. "Have you forgiven me yet, little sister?" he yells.

Ava puts in her earbuds and turns her music up loud.

It doesn't help. She can still hear Gregg laughing.

As Ava enters the school, she keeps the music at high volume. She slinks toward her locker. She keeps her eyes straight ahead. But she can feel the difference in the air around her. People are staring at her. How many of them have seen the parrot posts? Everyone in the whole school, it seems.

Ava's BFFs, the two Kims, grab Ava. One on each side. They hug and squeeze her. She pulls out her earbuds.

"That parrot is disgusting!" Kim B. says.

"Like, super gross!" Kim V. agrees.

Kim B., Kim V. and Ava. Best friends since preschool. But both Kims seem to have turned into beautiful swans. Ava feels like the ugly duckling beside them. The Kims smell like perfume, and both have perfect makeup and hair. Where did they even learn to do all that?

And both of them are wearing ankle boots, black leggings and silky tops, as if they planned their outfits together.

But the thing Ava is most jealous about is that both Kims still have their dads at home.

She sighs.

"Why did you get a parrot?" Kim V. asks.

"I didn't *get* it. I inherited it. From my great-uncle. Some guy I don't even remember." Ava puts her bag into her locker and takes out her binder.

Two boys in their grade, Hamid and Charlie, flap their arms as they pass by. "Bird lady!" one of them shouts.

Kim B. giggles. "He is sooo cute," she says.

"Who? Charlie?"

"No!" both Kims gasp.

"Hamid, of course," Kim V. says, batting her eyelashes as she looks over at him.

"Right," says Ava. "Of course." She doesn't really see it, but whatever. The three of them walk toward their first class, social studies. Ava ignores the bird calls and jokes that fill the air around her. She slumps in her seat. She is surprised when the two Kims grab seats in the row behind her.

"What's going on, guys?" Ava asks, turning around. "We always sit together."

Kim B. says, "Just…you know…" She glances at the other Kim. "The bird thing."

"What?" Ava asks.

"Well, it's kind of gross," says Kim V.

"But the bird isn't even here!" Ava cries.

The Kims both laugh at that. Just then their teacher, Mr. Patel, walks into the class. Ava has to turn back and face the front. The empty seats on either side of her make her want to sink into the floor and disappear. She knows no one is listening to Mr. Patel, that everyone is focused on the parrot.

When Mr. Patel turns to write some notes on the smartboard, Ava glances at her phone.

@gobigorgohome Why did you take the parrot pics down? We want more. @HamidManAboutTown We want more Mervin! HAHAHAHAHA

Ava sighs. This will all be over soon. In a couple of days, everyone will move on and forget those pictures were ever there. She hopes. She is so busy looking at her phone, she doesn't notice the girl sliding into the seat beside her.

"Hi," the girl whispers. "I'm Melinda Flores."

"Hey," Ava says, still looking at her phone.

"I thought you might like some company."

Ava puts the phone down. "Yes. Thank you. Are you new?"

"Um, I started here at the beginning of the year. But we haven't really met properly."

"Oh." Ava can't think of anything else to say. This girl is being so *nice* to her. Ava's life is such a nightmare, and her friends have abandoned her. But this stranger is being kind.

Melinda has long, silky hair. She has quick, bright eyes and a huge smile. She says, "I love parrots."

"Right." So that's why Melinda is sitting next to her. It's because of the stupid parrot. Another person reminding her of the stupid bird and the way her life has fallen apart.

Mr. Patel leans over. "Girls, no talking, please. You should be starting to plan your personal project. You need to choose a subject that interests you. You need to research it, make a presentation poster and present your topic to the class. And remember, no phones in class unless for research, right?"

"Sorry, Mr. Patel," say Melinda and Ava at the same time.

Ugh. The personal project. The only thing Ava's really interested in is online celebrities. Yikes! She tries to come up with an idea, but she's just too stressed.

At the end of class Melinda tries to talk to Ava again. But Ava gets up and walks away from her and from the two Kims. She avoids them and keeps her head down for the rest of the long, awful day. With every step she takes, with every birdcall in the hallways, Ava becomes more determined to get rid of Mervin.

A tiny part of her feels bad. Looking after Mervin was her great-uncle's last request. But then Ava remembers the feeling of Mervin's claws digging into her scalp. No. The bird has to go.

In her last class, Ava pulls out her phone and glances at it under her desk. She ignores all the notifications on the screen. Instead, she looks up the information for the zoo.

"Ava! This is not the time or the place for your phone!" yells Mrs. Miller. She is not even an old teacher, but she has issues with any technology. "You know my rules!"

"I was just—" Ava begins.

Mrs. Miller rants on about cell phones. "If I see it again, you'll be in detention!"

Ava has never had detention. Ever. She can hear the class laughing behind her. Around her. She feels tears spring to her eyes. Ava sinks her head into her hands. She has a horrible feeling that her day is only going to get worse.

Chapter Four

While she's walking home, Ava calls the zoo. After being on hold for ages, she gets put through to "Animal Recovery." At first they are reluctant to talk to her. Apparently people phone them all the time wanting to give them their unwanted parrots. Ava feels bad. Poor parrots.

The person on the other end asks Ava what type of parrot she has. "Um.

I'm not sure…" What the heck did the delivery guy call it? "Oh! I remember. It's an African gray. That's it!"

"Interesting. We actually are looking for an African gray. Our zoo doesn't have one. They are terrific mimics." The guy laughs as if he's said something funny. "Can your parrot mimic?"

"Talk, you mean? Yes. Yes! He definitely can. Does that mean you want him?"

"Okay. Well, maybe. We will have to set up a time with our bird specialist."

A bird specialist? What a horrible job, thinks Ava. "Great," she says.

"Someone could come by later this week."

"Later this week? Not today?" Ava asks.

"Not today, no. We're all booked up. Sorry."

Ava gives the man her contact details, then ends the call. She expects to feel better, but she feels miserable. And it's a miserable, cold afternoon.

When Ava gets home neither Gregg nor her mom is there. She slumps on the living-room sofa. Normally on Mondays she works out with an online class. But she just can't be bothered today. She sighs.

The living room is very clean and tidy. The whole house is like that. It used to be full of stuff, regular "people live here" stuff like books and knick-knacks and framed photographs. But after their dad left, their mom got obsessed with "decluttering." She has always been tidy. She has always been a perfectionist. But before, everything in their house was cozy and beautiful. Suddenly their mom got into reading blogs and watching videos about the minimalist lifestyle. Then she got rid of anything Dad had left behind. But she also got rid of the "art" that Ava and

Gregg had made when they were little. She donated all the books. She cleared away all the little keepsakes that had decorated the windowsills and shelves. Now, to Ava, the house feels empty and lonely. But her mom says it makes her feel peaceful. She says this is how the house was always meant to be.

Ava messages her dad.

Hey, Dad. How's it going?

Good. Missing my girl.

Maybe you could come back for a visit soon?

There is no answer for a while. Then her phone blips.

We'll have to see, Ava. Things are busy with my new job. I'm sorry, baby girl. I do miss you.

Sure, Ava thinks. If he were missing her, maybe he shouldn't have moved to Vancouver with his girlfriend. Sometimes she wants to see him so badly, she gets mad at herself. And it seems like every time she contacts him, she ends up feeling worse.

She hears the bird screeching from her room. "MONKEY! MONKEY! MONKEY!"

Argh. The last thing Ava needs right now is Mervin. She stomps into the kitchen and makes herself a protein drink. Another one of their mom's new fads. Super-healthy eating. She was even into cleanses for a while. Gross. Ava hated that. Now there is never anything decent to eat in the house. But this protein drink tastes pretty good— vanilla chai.

She takes a selfie, holding the drink awkwardly in one hand. After three or four shots, she gets a picture that looks okay.

A post-workout drink. I love getting healthy. Life couldn't be better. #getfit #lifegoals #proteinshake #lovinglife

Okay. She knows she's lying about working out. But posting how her day should have gone makes her feel better. Tomorrow she'll exercise. For sure.

@musicloves Where's the parrot, girl?

@tothemoon We want Mervin! How is that amazing bird today? #loveyourfeed #wherearemervinandavapics?

@melindaflor happy to talk to you about parrots

Ava lets out a scream of frustration. She chucks her phone onto the sofa. She hears a scream from her bedroom. Just like her scream.

The stupid parrot! He is copying her. *Again*.

She flings open her bedroom door. Her room stinks! It smells like straw and feathers and bird poop. She gags.

"You are a gross bird!"

"GROSS BIRD," Mervin replies. He cocks his head.

"You have ruined my life!"

"RUINED MY LIFE!" Mervin repeats.

Even though she knows he's only saying what he hears, she wonders if it's true. Has she ruined Mervin's life? His life has been turned upside down too. One day he was living with his beloved Bertie. And then suddenly he was here. In a new house. With new people.

Ava softens her voice. "Poor bird. It's been a big change for you too."

Mervin opens his beak and lets out a loud laugh. It's Gregg's laugh. He has copied it perfectly. Mervin laughs over and over. It's like Gregg is in the room. Argh. Just when Ava was starting to feel sorry for the horrid bird, he does something like that.

"Well," she says, "you don't need to worry. Our nightmare is going to be over soon. I called the zoo. So you better behave when they come to do an inspection. If all goes well, they'll take you away. And both of us will be happy." Ava stops talking. What is she doing, talking to this parrot like he can understand her?

Her phone buzzes. It is Kim B. texting.

I thought you were done with posting parrot pictures. Gross.

I am done! Ava replies.

What's this then? @avaandmervin

Oh no. What is going on? Ava opens up her social media and discovers both parrot pictures from yesterday under the name AvaandMervin. Oh my god! Gregg must have created the account. And it already has over *3,000* followers!

She checks her own feed. She has been unfollowed by lots of people.

She has only 521 followers now. Fewer than she had before Mervin arrived!

She calls Gregg. She can hear his phone ringing somewhere in the house. He must be home.

"What are you doing?" she yells, both into the phone and into the air.

He sticks his head around her doorway. He is holding his phone. "You're calling me?" His eyes are dancing. He is trying hard not to laugh. If Ava had something in her hand other than her phone, she would throw it at his annoying face.

"Why would you set up a social media feed about me and the parrot? Are you trying to ruin my life?"

"Little sister, I'm doing you a favor. You just don't realize it yet."

He walks across her room to Mervin's cage. "You're a good-looking guy," he says to the bird.

"GOOD-LOOKING GUY!" the bird replies.

Gregg laughs.

The bird mimics him. Laughing.

"Get out of my room!" shouts Ava.

"GET OUT, GET OUT!" Mervin yells.

Gregg leans forward and opens the cage.

"NO!" Ava shouts. "What are you doing?"

But it's too late. Mervin is out of the cage and flapping around the room. Laughing like Gregg.

Ava screams. Gregg has his phone out. It looks like he is filming. She lunges at him. Mervin swoops by.

Mervin lands on Ava's bookshelf. He scrabbles at the wood with his clawed feet. He knocks over a ceramic sculpture her mom put there. It shatters on the floor.

Then Mervin poops. "MONKEY IDIOT!" he yells.

Ava can't get the phone away from Gregg. He holds it up like he's still filming. She tries to calm herself. People could be watching this right now. Like, lots of people.

"So," she says, plastering on a fake smile, "if any of you have any advice on what to do to help me get Mervin back into his cage, I'd love to hear it."

Gregg hoots with laughter. "You are, like, the Parrot Girl! Oooh. Melinda Flores is watching, and she says, *Try offering him a treat.*"

Ava realizes that advice is from the new girl in class. She grits her teeth. "What a wonderful idea," she says sweetly. "What sort of treat does a parrot eat?"

"You even rhyme!" Gregg cries. "Keep it up, little sister. This is internet gold! Melinda writes, *Peanuts might work.*"

Ava keeps her fake smile on and marches from her room. Gregg follows. She keeps her back to him. And she doesn't scream when the bird flaps over her head. Mervin is coming along too.

"MONKEY IDIOT!" Mervin screams.

Ava is going to find some peanuts and try to end this nightmare.

Chapter Five

With peanuts and patience, Ava finally got Mervin back into his cage. Now she lies in her bed, the blankets pulled over her head to block out the sound of him scratching. Mervin mutters quietly. But the sounds he's making don't sound like words.

Ava checks her phone. Now there are 4,314 followers. For AvaandMervin.

Barely five hundred for Ava. Gregg, of course, posted the video and some photos too. The video has had the most likes so far. Ava watches it again. Mervin yelling, "MONKEY IDIOT" over and over while Ava frantically searches for peanuts. When she finally finds a tub of them, Mervin flies over and lands on her head. Ava screams. In the video. In real life, she plonks her phone facedown on the bed.

Ugh.

Despite the noise Mervin is making, Ava eventually falls asleep. She dreams of her family—Ava and her dad and her mom all together. She startles awake. In the darkness of her room, she has the feeling she is being watched.

The feeling creeps her out. Who could be watching her?

"Hello, pretty."

Mervin. Of course. Ava had forgotten about the dumb bird. She flips her phone over. It is packed with notifications for AvaandMervin. By the low blue light of the screen, she can see Mervin looking over at her. He has his head cocked and is watching her with one yellow eye.

"Hello, Pretty Pretty," says Mervin.

"Hello, you horrible bird," Ava says.

Mervin stares at Ava. She feels bad for being so mean.

"Sorry. I didn't mean it. You're not a horrible bird. I just had a bad dream, and it put me in a grumpy mood."

Mervin cocks his head again. It's like he's actually listening.

Ava finds that she wants to keep talking to him. "I mean, it wasn't a *bad* dream. It was a good dream—I was dreaming that me and my parents were having breakfast together. It was nice. But really they just fought all the time. It's probably a good thing that Dad left. I just miss him, you know?"

"Idiot," Mervin says quietly.

Ava giggles. "Dad is a bit of an idiot. It's true. He left me and Gregg behind. That makes me feel sad." Ava's eyes fill with tears. "But I think he's probably happier now. I should go to visit him. I wish Mom were happier too. Since he left, she hasn't really been herself. It's almost like she's afraid to be happy."

"Monkey," says Mervin. "Peanut?" he adds, sounding hopeful.

"Sure, have a peanut." Ava reaches over and opens up the tub. She passes him a peanut through the bars. He takes it gently with his beak and is soon crunching happily.

"You're actually a good-looking parrot," says Ava. "I mean, you have nice feathers."

Mervin laughs. He sounds like Gregg.

"But *that* is annoying. You have to learn to laugh like someone else. My brother is the worst."

"Worst," Mervin says.

"Exactly." Ava suddenly feels silly for talking to a parrot. "Good night, Mervin." She cuddles into the pillow. Her eyelids get very heavy.

"Ava," says Mervin quietly.

"Did you say something?" Ava mumbles as she drifts off to sleep.

In the morning, when Ava wakes up, she immediately looks over to the cage. Mervin's eyes are closed. Ava tiptoes out of her room. Her mom is in the kitchen, wiping the counter.

"I had to clean bird poop off the counter this morning, Ava," she says, frowning.

"Morning, Monkey Face," Gregg says. He pops his head up from the sofa.

"Sorry, Mom," Ava says. Then she turns to give her stupid brother a look.

"That bird has to go," says their mom. "It can't stay here. You don't know how to look after it properly. The house smells like parrot. And bird poop on the counter is unsanitary."

"You need coffee, Mom," says Gregg.

Their mom lets out a sharp breath, between clenched teeth.

Ava says, "I've already called the zoo. They're coming by later this week to assess him."

"Right. Good." Their mom wipes the already clean counter again.

"You called the zoo?" Gregg asks. "But what about a dying man's last wish?"

"Shut up, Gregg," says Ava.

"And your followers! They love you. You're a superstar."

"Gregg, I mean it. Shut up!" Ava yells.

"The bird is leaving our house, and that's that." Their mom picks up a mug and fills it with coffee. "The two of you need to stop fighting. I've had it up to here." She gestures with one hand to somewhere way above her head. "I'm off to my meeting."

Gregg looks over at Ava as their mom slams the front door. "Don't ask me what's up with her," he says. "She's been in a bad mood ever since Dad left."

Ava realizes that this is the first time either of them has mentioned their dad since he left.

"Do you miss him?" Ava asks.

"I kind of hate him, to be honest," Gregg replies.

For a brief second Ava adores her brother. Then he says, "At least now Dad can watch you on the internet. Pretend like he has a daughter."

Ava's warm and fuzzy feelings toward Gregg vanish. "You are such a jerk," she says. "Just take the stream down."

"You must be joking!" He grins. "You are going to be world-famous, little sister. People love this stuff! We can't take it down. We have a duty to serve the parrot-loving public." He hoots with laughter. Ava hears the echo of Mervin in her bedroom, laughing just like Gregg.

"Which is why you cannot let the zoo people come over," Gregg continues. "They can't take Mervin away. What will your fans think?"

"I'm a big joke to everyone, Gregg. Why don't you understand that?"

He laughs. "I am doing you a favor, Ava. But you don't realize it. Plus I'm driving you crazy at the same time. Perfect!" He vaults over the sofa and heads toward Ava's bedroom.

"What are you doing?" she yells, following him.

"Uh, what do you think?" He takes out his phone and starts filming.

He begins to narrate the video in a big voice. "And now let's see what happens when we let Mervin out for breakfast. Oh." Gregg spins around and holds the phone to film Ava. "Here she comes. The parrot whisperer!"

Ava wants to scream at him, but now she's on camera. She grits her teeth and walks as quickly as possible toward her room. "Let's not wake Mervin," she says in her calmest voice.

Gregg turns the camera back around. "Oh, look, he's awake, Parrot Girl! Hello, Big Birdy!"

"Hello, Monkey Idiot," Mervin replies to Gregg.

Ava can't help but smile at that. Then she hears the flap of Mervin's wings. Oh no, not again!

Chapter Six

Letting Mervin out is a bad idea. He makes a huge mess, and Gregg and Ava are going to be late for school. They finally get the noisy bird back into his cage with the promise of peanuts and then race to school. They arrive well after first bell and, of course, bump right into Mrs. Miller. Ava is sweaty, and her hair is all over the place. Gregg looks ridiculously perfect.

"Get to class, you two. Next late and you'll both be in detention."

Gregg grins, and Ava runs to social studies. That's twice in two days that she's been threatened with detention! Her life is falling apart.

Mr. Patel is talking about their personal projects when she arrives in class. Ava still has no ideas. She's not interested in anything. She looks around. Other kids are working on projects about Paris during the war, or homelessness, or recycling and composting, or even hip-hop. Lots of amazing and cool topics. She puts her head on her desk. Why can't she think of anything?

When Mr. Patel isn't looking, Ava checks her phone. Oh no! Gregg has posted the video from this morning. In it, Ava is flustered and waving her arms as Mervin flies around their house.

Gregg paused the video just as Ava started to yell. He's done some stupid replay on that moment. It's getting like after like after like.

Ava swallows back tears. She catches Melinda looking at her. Ava dips her head down—she doesn't want anyone seeing how upset she is.

"Hey, Parrot Girl," Kim V. says from the row behind. She snickers.

Ava doesn't reply.

"What's up, parrot lover? You missing your bird?"

Ava spins round. "You're supposed to be my BFF!"

"Come on, Ava. No one our age actually says that, right?"

"We do," Ava says in a small voice.

"Anyway, I'm just kidding. Wow. Calm down. You're not crying, are you?"

Melinda leans over and interrupts. "You aren't being a very good friend to Ava. Just leave her alone."

"Who are you to tell me about being Ava's friend?" Kim V. snaps.

"Yeah," Kim B. says. "Weirdo."

"Just leave us both alone," Melinda says.

It's not a snappy or a cool comeback. Melinda looks a bit like she might start crying too. But Ava feels a surge of gratitude. "Melinda is right," she says. "Leave us alone."

At the end of class, both Kims storm off. But Ava hardly notices. She's busy packing up her bag. And who cares what those girls think anyway? She sighs. She cares. Of course she does. She's been friends with them forever. And now they're not even talking to her.

"Are you okay?" Melinda asks.

"I guess." Ava shrugs.

Melinda is smiling. She gives off a feeling of being very calm and kind.

Ava finds herself wanting to talk to her. "Thanks for your help with the peanuts." Ava pauses. "I don't know much about parrots."

Melinda laughs. "Yeah. I figured."

"It's that obvious, huh?" Ava says, laughing a bit too.

She picks up her bag, and the two girls fall into step together. "My great-uncle gave me the parrot," she says. "He wanted me to look after it when he died. I guess I did love the parrot when I was a kid." Ava lets out an embarrassed laugh. "But the thing is, I don't even *like* him. He's smelly and gross and loud. And he's making a fool out of me."

"You don't like Mervin?" Melinda frowns. "See, I don't think that's true. I saw you online. I know you were screaming and yelling, but you were also trying to calm him down. You went hunting for peanuts."

"I guess you're right. And it was nice having Mervin in my room last night. I just don't know what I'm doing with him."

"Soooooo…" Melinda says as she expertly does a dance spin.

Wow, Ava thinks, this girl really doesn't care what other people think. Spinning circles in the school hallway like they're at a dance camp! Ava wonders when she herself started to care so much about what other people think.

"Soooooo what?" Ava asks.

"Soooooo, my parents used to have a parrot. His name was Fernando. He was a cockatoo. I grew up with him in our house, and I taught him a bunch of tricks."

"Tricks?"

"Yup. Fernando could step up and spin around and wave and say cute stuff.

It was adorable. But it also made him happy—he liked to do tricks. It kept him stimulated, so he wasn't bored. Right?"

"You think Mervin is *bored*?"

"I don't know. I've never met your parrot. But I think parrots are super smart and super interesting."

Ava thought about this for a minute. "Do you want to meet Mervin?" she asked. "I don't think he can do tricks. But maybe you can give me some tips on how to handle him."

"I'm happy to help."

"Come over then. I mean, if you're not doing anything after school."

"Let's see. I have chess club tomorrow, but I think I'm free today. I just have to let my mom know," Melinda says.

"That would be awesome," Ava replies. "Let's meet at the gate after last class and walk home."

Melinda pulls out her phone. "Here's a clip of Fernando pushing a ball," she says a bit shyly.

The girls pause in the hallway. Ava watches the cockatoo pushing a ball through a maze.

"You really think Mervin could do that? That is so cute!" Ava cries.

"That is so *cute!*" someone repeats. It's Kim V. She walks toward them. "And you two are so cute!" she says. "How great that you have a new best friend now, Ava. Another parrot girl."

"At least she has something interesting to talk about," Melinda says.

"You two parrot losers deserve each other. I can't believe we were ever friends, Ava," Kim says. She glares at Ava and then marches away.

"Go and bore someone else," Melinda calls after her.

Ava stares at Melinda, who is proudly standing up for her.

Ava watches Kim V. walking away. Maybe Kim V. is right! What *is* Ava doing? How did she become the girl who loves talking about parrots?

Suddenly Ava feels awkward and embarrassed. "Yeah. I have to go," Ava says. "I'll, um, see you later." She ducks her head down and quickly walks away.

Ava tries to ignore the parrot jokes and squawks for the rest of the day. She doesn't have any other classes with Melinda, but both Kims are in her afternoon classes. But they aren't talking to her at all.

By the end of the day Ava has a headache. After last class she waits for Melinda at the gate. She checks her phone. It's been ten minutes. Perhaps Melinda isn't coming after all. Ava wonders if Melinda is upset about what happened in the hall earlier.

Ava sees Melinda running toward the gate. "Sorry, Ava. I was in science, doing a cool experiment. I lost track of time. I hope you weren't waiting long." She gives Ava a huge smile.

Wow, Ava thinks, this girl is just all heart and sunshine. She's happy that Melinda doesn't seem mad about Ava ditching her earlier.

"I wasn't waiting long, no," Ava says.

Melinda links arms with Ava as they leave the school grounds. "I have so many ideas for tricks we can teach Mervin! This is going to be great!"

Chapter Seven

The first thing the girls do when they get to Ava's house is get some snacks. Mervin yells, "IDIOT MONKEY!" a few times from Ava's room and afterward is quiet. Ava makes popcorn and then decides they need smoothies too. "We have to prepare ourselves for dealing with Mervin."

"Your house is beautiful," Melinda says. She sits on a stool by the breakfast bar.

"Yeah, my mom is an interior designer."

"It's so clean and tidy. There's so much space."

"Yeah. But I feel like she's tidied us out of her life."

Melinda looks at her, curious.

"I mean," Ava continues, "it's just that when my dad left, Mom got obsessed with decluttering, and she's just throwing everything away. Like, *everything*." Ava sighs. "Sorry. I have no idea why I'm telling you all this."

"When did your dad leave?"

"At the start of the summer. It was the worst. It's not like him and Mom were happy before that, but that was just our family, you know? Now Mom is working and stressed and *still* decluttering. I can't put anything down anywhere without her throwing it out. Gregg is acting like nothing ever happened—most of the time anyway. And now he's making all these videos. Ugh."

"He's your brother, right?"

"Yeah. You'll probably fall in love with him. To be honest, I think that's the only reason the two Kims stayed friends with me for as long as they did. They were crushing on my brother."

"Really?"

"Yeah. I guess they think he's good-looking."

Melinda frowns. "I've seen him at school. Sure, he's handsome, but he's being so mean to you right now."

Ava shrugs. "Brothers. What can you do?" She pushes the button on the blender full of frozen berries and yogurt. When she turns it off, Mervin makes exactly the same *whirr* sound as the blender. Both girls laugh. They take their smoothies and popcorn and head to Ava's room.

"PRETTY, PRETTY, PRETTY!" Mervin yells.

"He sounds very excited," Melinda says.

Ava opens the door. Her room is *trashed*! Books have been shredded, and there is parrot poop on her bed and straw all over the floor. The curtains have claw marks in the fabric. "Oh my god!" Ava yells. "How did you get out of your cage?"

Mervin flaps over and lands on her head.

"PRETTY IDIOT MONKEY!" he screeches.

"What have you done, Mervin?" Ava asks. "Get off my head!"

"Did you leave the cage open?" Melinda asks.

"I don't know! Maybe?" Did she? She might have. She *was* rushing this morning.

"Hey, pretty boy," Melinda says softly. "You want to step up?"

"STEP UP!"

Ava watches in the mirror as Mervin raises a foot from her hair. "How does he know how to lift his foot like that?"

"It's a simple parrot trick. Lots of owners teach the words *step up* to their parrots. I wondered if Mervin had learned some basics. He seems pretty smart." Melinda holds out her arm, and Mervin steps neatly onto her hand. Melinda rewards him with a peanut. He immediately gets to work opening the shell.

"Wow. That's amazing, Melinda. You make it look so easy."

Mervin cocks his head and stares with his beady eye at Ava. "SO EASY!"

Ava laughs. "But that doesn't stop my room from being a total mess."

When Mervin finishes the peanut, he turns his gaze on Melinda. She says, "How about turn around?"

Mervin looks like he's thinking hard.

Melinda holds a peanut next to Mervin's beak. As he turns to reach for it, she moves the peanut around his head. Mervin turns a full circle to get the peanut. "Good bird, Mervin," Melinda says.

Mervin's neck feathers fluff, and he makes a quiet cooing noise. Is he saying thank you? Ava wonders.

"Melinda, he's loving this!"

Ava pulls off the poop-covered comforter. She sits on her bed, no longer caring that her room is a mess. Mervin is awesome! With Melinda's help, he practices turning around a few more times. Then they work on waving. Mervin lifts a claw as they say hello. He is rewarded with peanuts.

After a while they take him into the bathroom and give him a bath. Mervin splashes water and flaps around the sink, as happy as a pig in mud. "Good bird," Ava cries, delighted. "He's so funny!"

"We can teach him to poop in his cage instead of on the floor," Melinda says when they finally get Mervin, stuffed with peanuts, back into his cage.

"Seriously?"

"There's a bunch of ways to do it. I've seen them online—we can try them, at least. He probably had a routine in his old home."

"Home," Mervin says.

Ava thinks he sounds a bit sad. She wonders if he misses Bertie.

"With the stress of this new environment," Melinda continues, "he hasn't learned what to do in your house. He'll probably get the hang of the rules soon. He is pretty smart."

"PRETTY SMART!" Mervin agrees.

"African gray parrots are actually the best mimics. And Mervin is obviously very good at it. Like, outstanding. Good bird," Melinda says and reaches through the bars to give Mervin a scratch under his feathers. Then she comes to sit next to Ava.

"He *is* a good bird," Ava agrees. "Although he wakes me up at night. Chatting!"

"You need to cover his cage at night—parrots need dark to sleep. You could use a sheet. If it's totally dark, he won't wake you up at night."

"Really?"

"Try it."

"I totally will!"

Just then Gregg appears at the doorway. He has his phone out. "Come on then, Ava, give us some of that parrot fun we all love!"

Ava sticks her tongue out at him.

"Hey, big guy," he says to Mervin. "You're a rock star."

"ROCK STAR," Mervin agrees. But he doesn't flap around. He sits quietly in his cage.

Gregg sighs. "Well, this isn't going to go viral. Mervin, where's the drama?" He puts his phone in his pocket. He looks at Melinda and says, "Who are you?"

"This is Melinda," Ava says. "My friend from school."

Melinda beams at Ava. "Hi," she says to Gregg. "By the way, I don't think it's very nice of you to keep posting about Ava when she doesn't want you to."

"Whoa." Gregg laughs.

"I just think it's mean," Melinda says softly.

Gregg clears his throat. For once he seems speechless. He makes a face at Ava. "What happened to the Kims? I haven't seen them here for a while."

Ava shrugs. "Melinda knows a lot about parrots."

"Right," Gregg says. "Well, uh, yeah, good to meet you, Melinda." He backs out of the room. Ava looks at Melinda, who gives her a little smile.

"I can't believe you said that to him," Ava says. "All my friends are always trying to impress Gregg. Because, you know, they all think he's so hot."

It's Melinda's turn to shrug. She says, "I like guys who are nice."

Ava bursts out laughing. "Well, I don't know that Gregg knew what to do with himself. He's used to girls falling all over him."

Melinda falls back onto the bed, laughing. "Not. My. Type," she says.

After Melinda goes home, Ava sits down in the living room. She poses on the couch, trying to get a good shot. She lifts her arm to change the angle, wishing for the millionth time that she had a selfie stick. Finally, after a few attempts, she is happy with the photo and posts.

Relaxing at #home. Lucky to have a new friend @melindaflor. I want to build my following here—like if you want to help me. #lifegoals

After a few minutes her phone pings.

@musicloves Where's the parrot?

Ava rolls her eyes. She gets up and goes to the kitchen to make herself a bowl of noodles for supper. Gregg comes out of his room. "Food! Where's mom?" he asks, rubbing his tummy.

"You sound like Mervin. Make your own food. Mom isn't home from work yet."

"Is your prissy friend gone?"

"She's not prissy. She just doesn't like you."

"Yeah. Well, I don't like her either."

Gregg leans over the counter and picks up Ava's phone. He reads:

@futurefantasy WE WANT TO SEE THE BIRD! That would grow your list.

Gregg bursts out laughing. "I told you! They love it. They want Mervin."

"Don't touch my phone!"

"I was just telling you what your fans say. You only have *one* like, Ava."

"I only just posted!" she said.

Gregg laughs again. "It's your prissy friend who likes your post. Everyone else wants the parrot."

Ava tries to grab her phone. She knocks over the bowl of noodles. Hot water spills over the counter and onto Gregg, who leaps up. "Watch it, Ava!"

The front door opens. It's their mom. "You two are always shouting at each other. Can't you both just grow up?" She closes her eyes for a long moment. When she opens them, she says,

"It would be nice to come home to a bit of peace and quiet."

She walks down the hallway toward her room. She passes Ava's open doorway. "Oh, Ava. What is going on here?"

"I'm going to clean up. I just haven't got around to it."

"That bird needs to be out of my house," she says. "Now."

"He's doing way better, Mom. We can train him."

Ava is shocked to see that her mom is nearly in tears. "Please, Ava. Not now. I've had a really long day."

Ava looks at her mom's face. She can tell she's exhausted. "Mervin will be gone soon, Mom," she says. "The zoo person is coming over to assess him. It's just until the end of this week. I'm really sorry."

Her mom wipes her eyes. "It's just been a very busy day, honey. I need to change. I have to go back out. You two can figure out supper, right?"

Gregg nods. "Sure, Mom. We're good. Sorry."

As their mom disappears into her room, Gregg slides Ava's phone back over to her. "Sorry, Ava."

"I'm sorry too," she says. But Ava is distracted. She is thinking about Mervin and the zoo coming to take him away. She is surprised that the idea of the noisy, messy bird leaving makes her feel sad. "I better go clean my room."

Chapter Eight

At lunch the next day at school, Ava sits by herself at a table under the trees. It is warmer today, and the sun is shining. But Ava is feeling blue. And she forgot to pack herself a lunch. Being hungry doesn't help her mood.

She gets a text message:

This is Peter, the bird specialist from the zoo. I'd be happy to come over on

Friday. How is 4 p.m.?

Ava pauses. She remembers her mom's face the night before. She messages back.

Perfect.

She should feel happy, but she feels like crying. She sighs. She looks up and sees Kim B. heading her way, smiling.

"Look, Ava, I was thinking," Kim B. says as she slides in next to Ava. "It's stupid that we're fighting."

"I'm surprised you're even talking to me," says Ava. "Did Kim V. send you?"

Kim B. shrugs. "She feels bad. I feel bad. We're friends. We can figure this out."

"Well, I guess."

Kim wrinkles her nose, something she's done for years—Ava remembers her doing it when they were little. It means that Kim is trying to figure out what to say.

"You're both giving me a really hard time about this parrot," Ava says to fill up the awkward silence.

"Well, it is *super* gross."

Ava thinks about Mervin and how quickly he'd responded to Melinda's gentle voice. "I know he seems gross, but he actually isn't."

Kim B. wrinkles her nose again. Now she's disgusted—Ava knows Kim so well. "We don't want to talk about your parrot, okay?"

"I really appreciate you coming over, Kim," says Ava. "I hate it when things are awkward between us. But I do kind of like the parrot. Maybe you should come over and meet him sometime."

Kim B. shakes her head. "No way. But as soon as he's gone, can we come over?"

Ava doesn't know how to respond. She's confused. She wants her friends back. Right? She says, "The zoo will probably take him away on Friday— they'll be assessing him, but he's so smart they'll want him for sure. I'm actually sad about it. I like Mervin. And he's my responsibility. My great-uncle trusted me to look after him. He knew I liked the bird."

"When you were a kid!"

"Maybe my great-uncle saw something in me that I didn't even know was there."

"Whatever, Ava. At least the parrot is going."

Ava nods, but really she wants to shake her head. "I guess." Across the grass, Melinda waves at Ava. She starts to walk over. But Ava drops her gaze and pretends she hasn't noticed Melinda waving. Melinda isn't really the sort of person Kim B. wants hanging around. Ava looks up and sees that Melinda has changed direction—she is now walking toward another table. Ava feels her cheeks redden. She hopes Melinda will understand. Ava has to fix things with her BFFs.

Kim B. opens up her backpack and pulls out a granola bar. "How's Gregg doing?"

"Why?"

Kim B. giggles. "I don't know. Just wondering. It'll be good to see him next time we come over."

Ava asks, "Did you seriously just come over and talk to me because you think my brother's hot?"

"No!" Kim says.

"Oh my god. I've known you long enough to know when you're lying to me, Kim. You do this thing where you touch your eyebrow—just like that. Wow. You and Kim V. are welcome to my horrible brother. But not through me."

"You don't have to be like this, Ava."

"I thought it was weird that you came over to talk to me after what happened yesterday. Then I just figured that Kim V. had sent you."

"I'm not her puppet."

"So she *didn't* send you?"

Kim B. looks away.

Ava says, "She wants to hang out with Gregg. Well, maybe he'll ask you over sometime."

Kim B. gets up and flips her hair. "Whatever," she says and stomps away.

Ava slumps at the table. She takes out her phone and checks her feeds. There's been hardly any response to her last post, just requests for more photos of Mervin. And stupid Gregg has added another post to the AvaandMervin feed. That post has lots of likes and comments.

Ava flicks through the photos she took with Melinda the night before. There's a great shot of Mervin preening himself in the sink. She decides to post it.

My new #parrotpal @avaandmervin might be feathery but he's actually a bunch of fun. Now that he's figured out how to get clean, right @melindaflor ?

Almost immediately people start liking the photo and commenting. But Ava is waiting for Melinda to comment. She realizes she doesn't care about all the other likes and comments flashing on her phone. She just feels stupid for having ignored Melinda for Kim B.

But there is no comment from Melinda. Ava looks over at the table where Melinda is sitting. She's with people from the chess club. She doesn't even glance Ava's way.

That night both Gregg and Mom are out. Ava eats supper tuned in to Netflix. Mervin sits on the arm of the couch. He comments and clucks along. Sometimes it sounds like he's laughing. Ava finishes eating and then practices tricks with him. He agrees with Ava, saying, "GOOD BIRD" more than once, and he enjoys his peanuts.

Neither Gregg nor Mom is home by the time Ava goes to bed. She looks at her phone for a while and reads through all the comments about the photo she posted. She says good night to Mervin. He is shuffling around his cage. He clucks and grumbles and says "IDIOT MONKEY" a couple of times. Ava is so sleepy that she ignores the feeling she has forgotten something. She drifts into a dream about being famous. She's arriving at a huge party.

In the dream, she realizes that she doesn't want to be at the party. She wants to leave and hang out with her family. In the dream, she sees a parrot flying above the party. She tries to get the parrot's attention. He can't hear her. People are surrounding her, trying to get autographs and yelling her name.

"AVA!" a voice yells. She wakes. Her phone is ringing. Where is it? She fumbles around the bed. "AVA!" the voice shouts.

She finds her phone. But she has missed the call. It was her dad.

"AVA!" It's Mervin yelling.

"Stop yelling, you silly bird. It's the middle of the night. It was just my phone." Ava messages her dad.

Everything okay? Was asleep.

He replies immediately.

Was just calling when I realized how late it was. Sorry. Always forget the time difference. Miss you, baby girl.

Okay. Night.

Mervin starts yelling again. "AVA, AVA, AVA, AVA, AVA, AVA!" He is hopping around his cage.

"What is it?"

The door flings open. "Why is that bird making so much noise?" Ava's mom is standing at the door in her dressing gown. She flips on the light.

Gregg stands next to her. He's wearing his boxer shorts. He scratches his chest. Ugh. He's like a gorilla. "Gotta keep it down, Mervin." He yawns.

"MONKEY, MONKEY!" Mervin yells. He flaps and screeches in the cage.

"It's my fault, Mom. Sorry," Ava says. She remembers what Melinda told her. "I didn't cover his cage—

I knew I'd forgotten something. My phone ringing set him off. Sorry." Ava turns to Mervin and says softly, like Melinda did, "Hey, calm down, buddy. It's okay." She reaches to open the cage, thinking she can soothe him better with a peanut. Mervin bursts out in a flurry of feathers. He swoops out and lands on her mom's head.

"What is going on?" she shrieks. "Get this bird out of my hair! NOW!"

"Mervin, shhh, shhh," says Ava.

Gregg starts to laugh, and Mervin copies him. Then Mervin hops over and lands on Gregg's head. He nips him on the ear. Gregg yells. He bats the air around his head. "OW, that hurt!" he yells.

Ava grabs her phone. She films Gregg as he tries to get Mervin off his head. Mervin keeps laughing and nips Gregg's other ear.

Now Gregg is running around in circles in his underwear, yelling. Mervin keeps laughing. And Ava keeps filming. Then she holds up a peanut and calmly calls him. "Come, Mervin." It is the trick Melinda showed her.

She keeps filming with one hand while Mervin flies over to her. He lands on her arm and grabs the peanut. He happily goes back to his cage to eat it.

Gregg yells, "What just happened? That bird bit me! Were you filming?"

"No, of course not," says Ava. "You were *annoying* him. He didn't bite you—he just gave you a little bird kiss!"

"It hurt."

"Everybody back to bed," says their mom. "The zoo people can't get here quickly enough, as far as I'm concerned. That bird needs to be out of my house."

"Okay, Mom. The zoo guy is coming

on Friday. Can't we just enjoy Mervin while he's here?" Ava says.

Gregg stomps off to his room. Their mom sighs. "Good night, Ava. Keep that bird quiet."

Ava plonks back on her bed and writes her post.

THIS is where it's happening. Hahahahahahaha! @Greggtheman1234 @melindaflor #avaandmervin

Then she attaches the video of Gregg running around in his underwear. She loves the end of the clip, where Mervin comes to her and the peanut. She watches the responses. Lots of people like the video, and within a few minutes it has 150 views! This is, as Gregg always says, *internet gold*. There is still nothing from Melinda though. Ava totally gets why Melinda is ignoring her now and regrets snubbing her earlier.

Or maybe Melinda is sleeping. Like a normal person! Like Ava needs to be. "Night, Mervin," Ava says and pulls the sheet over his cage.

"Night," he mutters.

"I actually wish I could keep you," Ava whispers. After tonight, she knows there is no way her mom will ever allow that to happen.

Mervin doesn't reply. Ava falls into a troubled sleep.

Chapter Nine

"What did you do?" Gregg yells. He bursts into her room and lands on her bed.

"Get off!" Ava screams.

"Take it down now." He pats around her pillows, looking for her phone.

"I'm not taking that down. EVER!" Ava yells.

Their mom runs into the room. "What is going on here?"

"Ava posted a clip of me. With that bird. It's been watched thousands of times!"

Their mom *laughs*.

Gregg and Ava stop fighting.

"Are you laughing, Mom?" Gregg asks. "You think this is a joke?"

Ava watches their mom lean against Ava's desk, laughing so hard that tears form in her eyes. "Oh, Gregg, honey. I'm sorry. It's just...you've been posting all kinds of pictures of Ava and the parrot. What did you expect?"

Gregg rubs his hand through his hair. He sighs and shakes his head, but Ava can see the beginning of a smile on his lips. "I guess it is kind of funny."

"I am sorry, Gregg," their mom says. But she's still laughing. "Can I see the video?"

"Seriously, Mom?" Gregg asks, but Ava can tell he's not mad anymore.

He's probably as happy as she is to see their mom *laughing*.

The three of them sit on the bed and watch the video together. Their mom howls with laughter again. Which sets off Ava and Gregg. Soon all three of them are laughing. Then Mervin, from under his cover, starts to make his laughing sound too.

Ava pulls off the cover so Mervin can watch with them. They watch the video again and again. During the third replay a text message comes in for Ava.

This is Peter from the zoo. I can actually come by around 4 p.m. today to assess your parrot. Would that work?

Today! He was supposed to come on Friday. Today is way too early!

All three of them see the text.

"Good," Gregg says.

But Ava wonders if he really means it. His voice seems a bit flat.

"Perfect," their mom says. "Once that bird is gone, we'll all get back to normal around here. Now, we all need to get going. I'll make us pancakes while you two get ready for school." She gets up and heads out of the room.

Gregg ruffles Ava's hair. "Good one, little sister. Pancakes on a school day!"

"Don't touch my hair," Ava replies. But she smiles.

"IDIOT MONKEY," Mervin squawks as Gregg leaves the room.

Ava checks her phone. There is still no like or comment from Melinda. And now Mervin will be leaving this afternoon. How did the day start so well but turn so terrible? At least she'll get pancakes with her family.

At school Ava sees Melinda by her locker. She forces herself to go and say hello.

Melinda chews on a strand of her hair. Her cheeks are red, and she avoids Ava's gaze.

"Look, Melinda," Ava says, "I'm really sorry about yesterday. I thought Kim B. was trying to be friends with me. I didn't know how to deal with both of you together. I'm sorry."

"I get that being friends with me is too embarrassing for you," says Melinda.

"No," says Ava. "I mean, yeah, that might have been what I used to think. But that was before I...I really enjoy hanging out with you and with Mervin. And I'm sorry."

Melinda pulls her hair from her mouth. "Thanks. I like hanging out with you too."

"Although Mervin is going to the zoo today."

"Really? You're not keeping him?" Melinda says. "Wow, Ava, for a moment there I thought you were actually turning into a nice person. I mean, I know you have a reputation for being someone who just wants to be famous and who only cares about yourself. But I can't believe you'd just get rid of a living creature like that."

"What do you mean, a reputation?" Ava asks, stung. "I'm not like that."

"You are! At least, you seemed like that online, but as I got to know you in real life you seemed way kinder. Mervin is an amazing creature. I thought you knew how lucky you were to have him. I saw that video you posted last night with your brother. You seemed to be having a great time. Then you posted a photo this morning of your family and Mervin having pancakes. It seemed like you were finally being real online. But none of it is true with you." Melinda shakes her head. "I'm so dumb. I thought we'd be great friends."

Ava is shocked. How did her apology go so wrong? "We will be. We are!"

Melinda slams her locker shut. "I've got to go. You're welcome to the Kims of this school. You guys suit each other. You're all fakes."

Ava watches Melinda storm away.

In social studies Ava sits alone. Melinda has moved back to her old seat, and the two Kims are whispering behind Ava. The others are working on their personal projects. Suddenly Ava knows what she is going to research. Parrots! African grays! She'll do a project on Mervin.

She opens up a search engine on her phone and begins to make notes. On a whim, she texts her mom and gets Great-Uncle Bertie's full name. She looks him up. Her mouth drops open. She's found a Wikipedia page all about him. She learns that someone wrote a book about him. She texts her mom to ask if they can buy the book. She learns that Great-Uncle Bertie fought in North Africa during World War II. After that he traveled and worked as a naturalist throughout Africa. He even discovered various species of birds and plants!

And then, right there online, she finds the story of Mervin! There's even a picture of Mervin and Bertie. He found Mervin as a baby parrot, sick and with no feathers. He figured that Mervin's mother had been killed or captured. But he waited to see if she would return. When the parrot's mother never came back, Bertie nurtured baby Mervin to health. Mervin ended up traveling all over the world with Bertie. Ava learns that in those days it was easier to travel with animals. And Bertie did a *lot* of traveling.

The bell rings. Class has passed so quickly. Everyone packs up and starts heading out of the room.

Mr. Patel comes over. "I was happy to see you working so hard on your project, Ava. You sure made a lot of notes."

She looks at the pages in front of her. She has written loads. "Yes," she says. "I thought I was going to do a project about African gray parrots, but I think I'm going to do a more personal project. All about my Great-Uncle Bertie and his travels. And his parrot. Mervin is a great bird. Great-Uncle Bertie left him to me in his will."

"That's so interesting, Ava," says Mr. Patel. "I look forward to your presentation. Maybe you could even bring Mervin to class with you when it's your day."

"Sure!" says Ava. And then she remembers. The zoo is coming to take Mervin away this very afternoon.

Chapter Ten

Ava rushes home from school. She opens the front door. Her mom calls out, "Hey, honey! I was hoping you'd be back." She waves.

Ava stands in the doorway. "What are you doing home?"

Her mom shrugs. "I wanted to say goodbye to Mervin."

"About that, Mom…I was wondering if we could think about—"

Gregg pushes past Ava into the house. "The feathery guy's still here?"

"Why are you both so concerned about seeing Mervin? You don't even like him!"

Ava walks inside and drops her backpack. She heads to her room. Before Gregg interrupted, she had almost asked her mom if she could keep Mervin.

When Mervin sees Ava he calls out. "Pretty!"

Ava gets him out of his cage. He puffs his feathers and clucks, rubbing his beak against her cheek.

"Hey, buddy."

Her phone buzzes. It's a message from Peter from the zoo.

Running late. I'll be there closer to 5 p.m. Sorry.

Okay. No problem.

A whole extra hour with Mervin! She grabs the bag of peanuts and starts on the "turn around" trick.

Gregg and their mom come into her room. With Ava's help, Mervin performs a second turn around. He clucks happily and takes his peanut.

Their mom is surprised. "Look at what he can do!"

Gregg's phone rings loudly. His ringtone is a hip-hop track. Mervin squawks and starts bobbing his head. "He's dancing," Gregg says. He doesn't answer the call but instead holds up the phone.

Mervin bobs his head from side to side and starts moving his whole body in time to the music.

When the phone stops ringing, Gregg finds more music. Mervin jumps onto his head and starts dancing. Ava gets up and dances along. Soon their mom is dancing too. Ava takes out her phone and films them all dancing around.

Her phone buzzes. It's Peter from the zoo.

Managed to wrap things up. Am at the door. No one answering.

He's here! Ava leaves Mom and Gregg dancing with Mervin and answers the door. The man waiting outside is small with curly gray hair. He has a big smile. He shakes Ava's hand and says in his raspy voice, "So, where's the bird then?"

Ava leads Peter to her room. They stand in the doorway and watch Gregg and her mom dancing with Mervin. When they realize they are being watched, they both pause. Then they laugh. Gregg stops the music, and Mervin yells, "MONKEY MONKEY!"

Peter introduces himself and pulls out a clipboard. "So," he says, "I understand that looking after this bird is too much for you. That happens. I understand he was an inheritance. Amazing how long these creatures live."

"Yes, they can live up to eighty years," Ava says.

Both Gregg and her mom look at Ava. "Goodness, Ava, how did you know that?" her mom asks.

"I was researching parrots. For my project. Actually, I was researching Great-Uncle Bertie too, Mom." Ava takes a deep breath. It's now or never. "Look, I know Mervin is loud sometimes. And I know I'm just learning how to look after him—like last night when he woke you up because I forgot to put the cover over him. But I think I could do a better job."

Her mom holds up one hand. "Ava, what are you saying?"

"I know you don't like him, and he doesn't fit with our clean and decluttered house, and he's noisy and—"

"Ava!"

"I mean, I guess, I'm saying I'd really like to keep Mervin."

Her mom lets out a slow breath. "Are you sure? I mean, I'm impressed that you've learned so much about parrots. And I do like his tricks. But looking after an animal is a serious job."

"He is pretty awesome though, Mom," Gregg says.

Ava looks at her brother in surprise. "Really? Even when he bites you?"

"It was just a little nip," Gregg says. "Plus I, um, I like that the three of us are doing stuff together now."

Peter shifts his weight from one foot to the other. Waiting.

Their mom looks at them both. "The three of us doing something together?" she murmurs. She turns. "I'm sorry, Peter. It looks like we've wasted your time here. I think we might see if we can keep Mervin here for a while longer. How does a three-month trial period sound, Ava?"

"Really, Mom?" Ava throws herself into her mom's arms and hugs her tightly. It's the first time she's given her mom a hug in a while, Ava realizes. A big, full hug. She squeezes her mom, who squeezes her back.

Her mom says, "Maybe we don't need to get rid of everything, hey?"

Ava pulls back and sees that her mom has tears in her eyes. Mervin flaps over and lands on Ava's shoulder. He nuzzles against her neck.

"In these circumstances," Peter says, "when someone has called us in, we do like to be sure that the bird is being well looked after. To me, it seems a three-month trial period would be a good idea. Then I will come back and we can reassess together, okay?"

Ava nods. Mervin flies out of the room and perches near the front door. "BYE-BYE!" he yells.

Gregg laughs.

"I think Mervin is making himself clear," their mom says as they all follow Peter out to the hall. "Okay, you noisy bird, back to your cage while Gregg makes supper."

"While *I* make supper?" Gregg says. "Why me?"

Ava holds out a peanut and gets Mervin onto her shoulder. He nudges her cheek again. He really is cute!

Peter opens the front door. "I'll be off then. Good to meet you all. I'll see you again in three months."

Just then Melinda runs up the path to the front door "Don't take him!" she yells. She has both of her arms out. "My parents say that we can keep him at our house. Don't take him to the zoo, please!"

"Um, hello and goodbye!" Peter says and makes his way around Melinda. She looks confused.

Ava laughs. "Melinda! Mervin's not going to the zoo. We're keeping him here. Although if Gregg and I ever go to Vancouver to see Dad, then Mom might like it if Mervin stayed with you while we're gone."

"You're planning to go to Vancouver?" Mom says, slightly stiffly.

"Maybe during Christmas break, Mom," Ava says. "If that's okay? I haven't asked Dad yet."

Gregg changes the subject. "So, Melinda, are you coming in or are you just going to hang out there?"

Ava glances at Gregg. Funny! She can tell by how he's staring at her friend that he *likes* Melinda. Huh!

Melinda doesn't even look at him. "You're not getting rid of Mervin?" Melinda says to Ava.

"No. You were right."

"I was! But I was so mean to you. I'm sorry, Ava."

"No, I'm sorry. But Gregg's right. You should come in and hang out."

"Right. Yes," Gregg says. He's acting all formal and weird. "You're welcome to stay for supper too. Right, Mom?"

Their mom nods and introduces herself to Melinda.

"I should warn you," Ava whispers. "Gregg's cooking tonight." She and Melinda both giggle.

Ava, Melinda and Melvin head to Ava's room while Gregg figures out supper.

That night Ava takes out her phone. She looks through the photos and videos from that evening. She has a great photo of Mervin on Melinda's shoulder. She sends the picture to Melinda. Then she chooses the video of Mervin dancing to hip-hop. She posts:

My family has changed a lot over the last year. I haven't been truly honest with you about how hard that's been for me. And for our family. There haven't been breakfasts together. To be real, there hasn't even been that much communication between us. But when Mervin came into our lives, suddenly things started to change. He was noisy and weird and loud. But with the help of @melindaflor and @Greggtheman1234 I have learned a lot about how to handle this guy. Look at how he dances! And weirdly, having him here makes it easier for me to think about connecting again with my dad. Strange how that happens! Over the next while, I'm going to share a lot of stuff about #mervintheparrot and the man who saved him. @avaandmervin

Ava shares the video. She's never been so truthful online before. She wonders what people will think about the real Ava. Likes and positive comments start pouring in right away. Ava smiles. She puts her phone down and gets ready for bed. When she checks again she has 97 likes already and a bunch of new followers. More important than that, three people have commented that they've had a tough year too. One of them thanks her for sharing her family's story.

There's a flash of a notification. Kim V. Her comment isn't surprising:

Super gross

Ava finds that she doesn't care. She replies.

To each their own

She adds a huge smiling face and a heart.

Another comment pops up.

**@melindaflor Loving my new BFF
and her amazing parrot companion
#avaandmervin**

Ava puts a row of hearts in reply.

There is a quiet knock on the door.
Her mom comes in. "Sweetheart, I
wanted to say sorry."

"Why?"

Ava's mom sits close to her on the
bed. "I was clearing up too much,
getting rid of everything. I was sad,
and I didn't know how to deal with
that. I should have thought about how
to involve you and your brother more.
I've just been learning how to deal with
my new reality."

"You don't need to be sorry," says
Ava. She feels very grown up all of a
sudden.

"Well, I am. And I think you should
go visit your dad in Vancouver. I'll be
fine. I'm doing well now. Your dad and

I…we weren't happy. But now I can see myself being happy again." She leans in and hugs Ava.

Mervin says, very softly, "Home, home, home." Ava and her mom squeeze each other a little more tightly.

When her mom leaves her room, Ava messages her dad.

Gregg and I were talking about coming to Vancouver over the break.

Ava watches as three dots appear. She wonders what her dad will say.

I would love that, baby girl.

Ava smiles. She puts her phone on *silent.* Mervin, who has been quietly watching her, opens his beak like he is yawning.

She wonders how he will behave when she brings him to class. She can't wait to share her personal project with everyone. But she has a lot of work ahead of her. She knows that with

Melinda's help, she will be able to train Mervin so that he can come to school. She *hopes* he will behave himself! "Night, Mervin."

"NIGHT, MERVIN!" the bird replies. As Ava puts the cover over his cage, Mervin chuckles softly. "NIGHT, MONKEY!" he adds.

"Shh now, time for sleeping," Ava says.

"PRETTY AVA."

He *did* say her name!

Alice Kuipers has written many books for young people, and they have been published in dozens of countries. Her work has also been made into plays and produced for radio. She lives in Saskatoon, Saskatchewan. She once shared her home with a parrot named Fernando.

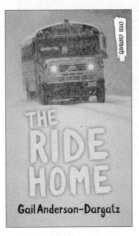

City kid Mark has come to a small town to live with his grandmother after his mom goes into rehab. He has to take a school bus home for the first time and quickly decides that all the kids on the bus are nuts and does his best to avoid interacting with any of them. But when the bus is involved in a serious accident, Mark has to work with a couple of other students to get everybody to safety.

Chapter One

I step into the school bus and stand next to the driver's seat, looking for a place to sit by myself. The bus smells like rotten oranges, sweaty running shoes and cheese. It's the middle of November, and this is my first time on the bus. In fact, this afternoon is the first time I've been on *any* school bus. Back in Vancouver I took public transit, the city buses.

And Gran dropped me off this morning on my first day at this school.

"Keep moving," the driver says. But she doesn't bother to look up from the romance novel she's reading. She's about as old as Gran, in her sixties. And she wears a fedora. Not just a hat. A *fedora*. Like, an old man's hat. I bet she's like that teacher I had in sixth grade who wore a different hat to school every day. A cowboy hat one day, a crown the next. Thinking she's being funny or *fun*. But at least that teacher had pizzazz, energy. This driver appears worn out, like she's been driving the school bus for a while now. Too long. She nods wearily in my general direction. "Take a seat."

Yeah, I think, but where? Most of the seats already have at least one kid in them. Super-little kids, probably kindergartners, sit in the first rows at the front, and what look like elementary kids are just behind them. The ones who look like they're around ten or eleven, younger middle schoolers, take up the middle of the bus. The biggest kids, the cool eighth graders, are at the back.

Seating on the school bus is by age group then, I guess. Well, except for this one girl who's clearly the weird kid. She's about my age, thirteen or so, but is sitting three seats from the front with the young kids. She is wearing glasses, and her hair is bunched into a knot. She has these big headphones on and is reading a book. I can see the title. It's a textbook on how the brain works. A smart kid then.

It's clear that everyone in each little group knows one another. They're friends. I'm arriving at this school late in the fall. Even if I wanted to, which I don't, I doubt I'll make friends now. Who cares? It's not like I'm staying long anyway.

I start to make my way down the aisle. A red-haired girl whispers to another girl, and they giggle at me like I've got my fly open or something. I check. I don't. I feel my face heat up.

"Hey, fresh meat!" some guy shouts.

"What's with the merman hair?" the red-haired girl asks. Oh, so it was my *hair* they were giggling about. There are a few dye jobs on the bus. But nothing like my bright neon green-and-blue spikes. I just had it done before…well, before.

I ignore them, keeping my eyes on the single empty seat I spotted at the very back. I want nothing to do with these rural freaks. I'm only staying with Gran until Mom gets back on her feet. Then I'm back to the city, first chance I get.